"Were you using magic?"

Clara almost had not dared to speak to the queen. But Queen Mab had asked her a question, and she could not let it go unanswered. "I was, Your Majesty," she'd said.

"The healing charm is very powerful, Clara Bell. Did you learn it from Tinker Bell?"

"I did, Queen Mab."

"Tink should know better than to teach that to you. It takes life to heal life."

Clara wasn't exactly sure what Queen Mab had meant when she said that. But she had curtsied deeply. "Forgive me, my queen," she'd said.

"Do not be ashamed, Clara Bell. You are a young fairy right now, but you have a gift for magic. You will be a very great fairy one day."

THE fairy bell SISTERS

Clara
and the
Magical Charms

Margaret McNamara

ILLUSTRATIONS BY JULIA DENOS

BALZER + BRAY
An Imprint of HarperCollins*Publishers*

Balzer + Bray is an imprint of HarperCollins Publishers.

Clara and the Magical Charms
Text copyright © 2014 by Margaret McNamara
Illustrations copyright © 2014 by Julia Denos

Library of Congress Cataloging-in-Publication Data
McNamara, Margaret.
  Clara and the magical charms / Margaret McNamara ; illustrations by Julia Denos. — First edition.
    pages cm. — (The fairy bell sisters) ; [#4]
  Summary: "Clara Bell needs to use her powers when she and Rowan, a gnome visiting Sheepskerry Island for the Valentine's Games, are faced with very serious trouble" — Provided by publisher.
  ISBN 978-0-06-222811-6 (hardcover bdg. : alk. paper)
  ISBN 978-0-06-222810-9 (pbk bdg. : alk. paper)
  [1. Fairies—Fiction. 2. Magic—Fiction. 3. Gnomes—Fiction. 4. Contests—Fiction. 5. Sisters—Fiction. 6. Valentine's Day—Fiction.] I. Denos, Julia, illustrator. II. Title.
PZ7.M47879343Ckr 2014   2013012324
[Fic]—dc23   CIP
                                                                         AC

Typography by Erin Fitzsimmons
15 16 17 CG/OPM 10 9 8 7 6 5 4 3 2
❖
First Edition

for

Donna Bell Bray

one

Valentine's Day for fairies is a lovely affair, as fairies like to send and receive valentines more than anything else. (Anything else in February, that is.) And Valentine's Week on Sheepskerry Island is better than anywhere else, because Queen Mab enchants Lady's Slipper Field and turns the dark of winter into the fresh breath of summer. All the Sheepskerry fairies gather in the meadow to exchange gifts and cards. They smell the orange blossoms and the roses. They throw off their heavy coats and scarves and mittens and wear their light summer dresses. They kick off their shoes and turn their faces to the warm sun.

Also, gnomes come.

Gnomes?

You didn't think there were only *trolls* in the world of the fairies, did you? (Trolls hibernate through the winter, by the way.) Gnomes are terribly different from trolls. Gnomes don't have warts, for one thing. They're not smelly. And they can talk properly, though they have a bit of a lilt to their speech as a result of living on  the faraway Outer Islands. I know you may have seen garden gnomes with long beards and fishing poles, still as statues at the bottom of a garden. That's what gnomes look like when they get old and grumpy. But when they're young—

"When they're young, gnomes are lots of fun," said Clara Bell as she knotted a warm purple scarf around her neck. It was a very cold February day, and all the Sheepskerry fairies were bundled up tight, especially Tinker Bell's little sisters.

two

I'm fairly certain you've met Tinker Bell's little sisters, but if you have not, let's please make their acquaintance now. Here are:

Clara Bell   Rosy Bell

Golden Bell

Sylva Bell

and baby
Squeak

The five Bell sisters—and their friend
Poppy Flower—were making their way back
from fairy school, which had let out early today,

as the snow was falling fast and thick. They darted between snowflakes as they flew.

"Gnomes *are* lots of fun," said Goldie, "even if too many of them wear those awful pointy hats."

"I like their hats!" said Rosy.

"Tutu!" said Squeak.

"Me three!" said Sylva. "And I don't mind what they wear as long as they're not too good at sports. Because I want to beat them all at the Valentine's Games."

That's another thing the fairies love about February: the Valentine's Games. I won't tell you about them now, as Rosy will tell us about them in a moment or two, *if* you can be patient.

"The only way you'd beat *all* the gnomes in your very first year of competition," said Goldie, "is if you used magic, which unfortunately we don't have much of yet."

"Not true!" said Sylva. "I've been training!

Besides, I'll have lots of magic soon."

"Not too soon, I hope," said Rosy. "We still have some growing up to do before we get our magical powers." Rosy gave Sylva a hug on the wing. "But I'm sure when you do you'll be as magical as Tink herself."

That made Sylva smile. And though none of her sisters saw it, Rosy's words made Clara smile, too. She wasn't ready to tell her sisters— yet—but she knew her magical powers were growing. She had been practicing her fairy charms since her last birthday, and she could already make a bell ring without touching it. (She was a Bell sister, after all!) Just last week, she'd taught herself how to make a rose bloom in the snow. Right now, she was working on her sparkle charm. That was a tricky one.

As Clara flew toward home, she thought about something that had happened long ago, when she was a very young fairy. She had noticed a tiny grasshopper in the tall grass near Lupine Pond. Its leg was broken, so it could not hop or even sing a grasshopper song to summon help. (Grasshoppers use their legs to make their songs!) Clara had known she didn't have a hope of helping the grasshopper—she hadn't even started learning charms yet at school. But she couldn't bear to see the injured insect. Then all at once, she recalled a charm she'd heard her big sister, Tinker Bell, recite once, long ago. How did it go?

Clear as crystal, Clara heard Tink's voice in her head. She closed her eyes, stretched out her arms, and said:

Harm and hurt
And pain no more.
Feel this power,
From my core.

May you be
Sound as a bell.
May my magic
Make you well!

Clara had felt faint and dizzy, and it took a few moments before she was well enough to open her eyes again. She steadied herself and looked at the grasshopper. It hadn't hopped away. It was exactly where she had first seen it. Her charm had failed!

But the very next moment she heard a tiny little *chirrp* coming from her grasshopper friend. That could only mean . . .

"Your leg has healed!" she'd cried.

Then she'd heard a voice behind her. "Clara. Clara Bell."

It was Queen Mab! Clara had nearly jumped out of her wings.

"Were you using magic?"

Clara almost had not dared to speak to the queen. But Queen Mab had asked her a question, and she could not let it go unanswered. "I was, Your Majesty," she'd said.

"The healing charm is very powerful, Clara Bell. Did you learn it from Tinker Bell?"

"I did, Queen Mab."

"Tink should know better than to teach that to you. It takes life to heal life."

Clara wasn't exactly sure what Queen Mab had meant when she said that. But she had curtsied deeply. "Forgive me, my queen," she'd said.

"Do not be ashamed, Clara Bell. You are a young fairy right now, but you have a gift for magic. You will be a very great fairy one day."

Clara could hardly believe her ears. "I will?" she'd asked in a whisper.

"Yes, Clara Bell, you will," Queen Mab had replied.

Clara had never forgotten that encounter with the queen. (Would you?) In fact, Queen Mab's words had given Clara great confidence her whole life.

However, I'd better warn you: If you're looking for a story where a very confident fairy sails along making clever decisions, always acting prudently, and never taking on more than she can manage, then this book will not be your cup of fairy tea. But if you'd like to hear about a fairy who's admired by all and expects so much of herself that she takes on far too much—so much that she almost risks her life—then you'll want to turn the page.

I'm keeping my fingers crossed you'll turn the page. . . .

three

W hew! I can uncross my fingers!

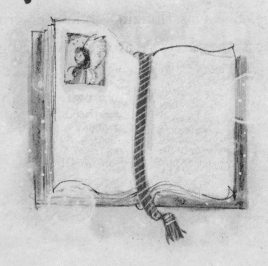

four

Clara tucked the memory of Queen Mab's words into a pocket of her mind and flew in the door of the Bell sisters' fairy house. She was thinking about her growing magic as the sisters sat around the fire together that evening.

"Rosy, I think you'd better finish your homework and stop writing that letter to Lulu," said Clara. "You're falling behind in Troll Tracks again."

"I just want to tell her about the Valentine's Games," said Rosy. Lulu was Rosy's friend—a real human child who believed in fairies (like someone else you might know). "I've written her about the sack races and the long jump and the three-legged race and the tossing of the branches." She looked over her letter. It was already four pages long. "Now I need to tell her about the swim round the island. I hope the dolphins join in again."

"There's a baby dolphin this year," said Sylva, who was trimming lace for valentines. "Have you seen her? She's getting so fast! Poppy and I have named her Speedy."

"That's a cute name," said Goldie.

"I know! Poppy wanted to name her Bluey but I told her my name was better."

"Bluey's nice too," said Rosy. "But whatever she's called, that little dolphin is the sweetest thing ever."

"Coomada!" said Squeak.

"Yes, we all love babies, don't we, Squeakie?"

said Clara. She gave Squeak a big hug and looked over at Goldie, who was deep in a pile of silk scarves. "How are Fairy Fractions going?"

"*Humph,*" said Goldie.

"I love Fairy Fractions," said Sylva. "Three-fifths of a starfish plus two-fifths of a starfish equals one whole starfish!"

"Very good," said Clara. "Goldie, since you're not doing your homework, can you please get Squeakie into her pj's?"

"Not right now," said Goldie. "I'm choosing a scarf to wear to the Games tomorrow." She picked one out from the pile. "This looks good with my sky-blue eyes, don't you think?" she asked the mirror, which did not reply. (Mirrors on Sheepskerry are not enchanted.)

Clara glanced at her sister and caught sight of her own reflection.

"You look nice tonight, Clara," said Sylva. "Did you polish your wings?"

Clara had not polished her wings. She had not changed a thing about herself. And yet her long, dark hair was shinier than ever. Her skin almost glowed. And her eyes, always a deep brown, seemed to be flecked with gold.

Perhaps her newfound magic was giving her a glow from inside.

five

"Oh my word! The meadow is *gorgeous!*"

"Queen Mab has done her *best* magic ever!"

The Fairy Bell sisters shook the snow from their wings and flew into Lady's Slipper Field. All the fairies were gathering there. This year the enchanted meadow was more lush and fragrant and flower-filled than ever before.

"I think the gnomes must have done some of this magical gardening," said Iris Flower. "It *is* their specialty."

"Off with this horrid winter hat!" Goldie

cried as she ran through the lupines. "Ooh! Avery!" she called to her best friend. "Can you feel that island sun?"

"Of course I can. It's a picture-perfect day!" said Avery.

"I must look picture perfect for when the gnomes arrive," said Goldie. "How do you like my skirt?"

"It's pretty, Goldie, but I don't think it will help you win any races," said Sylva. "Heigh-ho, Poppy!" she called. "Let's do some flying practice. There's no snow to weigh our wings down here."

"I'll take Squeak out of her fairy stroller," said Rosy. "She'll love being in her bare feet again. We'll go for a romp, won't we, Squeakie?" Rosy looked over at her older sister. "Do you have time for a quick walk, Clara?" she asked.

"No," said Clara. "I have too much work to do. I promised Queen Mab I'd organize the welcoming banquet and decorate the banqueting hall."

"You always take on so much," called Goldie. "Queen Mab's lucky to have you."

"We're all lucky to have Clara," said Rosy.

What Rosy didn't know was that Clara actually wanted to be by herself. It was the perfect time to practice her sparkle charm. Most of the island would be deserted, as everybody would be in the meadow for the opening ceremony—which meant there would be not a soul on Sunrise Hill.

Clara darted out of the summery meadow and away up the hill. She hoped no one would notice where she was going.

It was cold and snowy up on the hill, but she knew the chilly wind wouldn't trouble her if she could get some magic going. She had studied her Fairy Charms book last night, after all her sisters had fallen asleep. If she did this charm just right, the top of Sunrise Hill would be transformed.

Clara had memorized the words of the charm—that wasn't the hard part. It was doing the arm movements properly and spinning at the correct speed so that she always ended in the same spot. She closed her eyes and gave it a try:

Turn thrice around.
Fling wide your arm.
Sparkle now!
Obey my charm!

She opened her eyes—and started coughing. The pretty white snow of Sunrise Hill was covered in soot! "Where did all—*ack*—this come from? *Ack! Ack!*" Even the squirrels were covering their faces with their scrawny winter tails. "I must have done the spell all wrong!" Clara's eyes were streaming, and her nose was running. "I'm so sorry, little squirrel," she said. "I'd better clear this soot before Queen Mab thinks there's been a fire on Sunrise Hill. Sparkles will drive the smoke away—but can I do it?"

Clara stood perfectly still and quieted her cough. She thought of what Queen Mab had said to her: *You will be a very great fairy one day.*

Clara filled her mind with the idea of her magical power. And she recited the charm again:

Turn thrice around.
Fling wide your arm.

Sparkle now!
Obey my charm!

Tentatively, Clara opened her eyes. The black soot was gone. In its place was a shimmering curtain of golden sparkles. They floated down to the ground and dusted the pure white snow, making it shine more brightly than Clara had ever seen. They landed on tree branches and turned the dark bark into patterns of shimmering gold. They turned the sweet little squirrel's coat golden, from whiskers to tail. The sparkles made Sunrise Hill, always a beautiful place, look absolutely breathtaking.

"I can't believe it!" cried Clara. "Oh, how beautiful! I did it! My first sparkle charm!"

A distant cheer went up from the meadow, and Clara remembered—the welcoming banquet. She hadn't done a thing to get ready!

Six

Clara flew from Sunrise Hill back to Queen Mab's palace. Everyone would be descending there soon for a hearty dinner. She'd better get going—fast.

"Hey, Clara!" It was Julia Jellicoe. "You're going the wrong way!" Julia flew right into Clara's path. "The opening ceremony is almost over. Come on!"

"I'm not going, Julia," said Clara. "I have too much work to do." Clara hoped she didn't sound too prim. She couldn't exactly tell Julia that she'd been practicing her magic. Not when she hadn't mentioned it to her sisters—or to Queen Mab. "I've got to set up the welcoming banquet."

"Oh, thank goodness *somebody's* going to organize it," said Julia. "There are plates and dishes all over the place. Ours is a surprise."

"Ju-lia," said Clara. "What kind of surprise?"

"The gnomes will love it. See you later!"

When Clara arrived at the palace, her cheeks were red and her toes were freezing. She flew into the banqueting hall and warmed up by the fire. Then she went into the kitchen and looked over the chart she had put up last week, just to make sure everyone had done her part.

"Oh dear me no!" she said. "They've done exactly what they said they wouldn't."

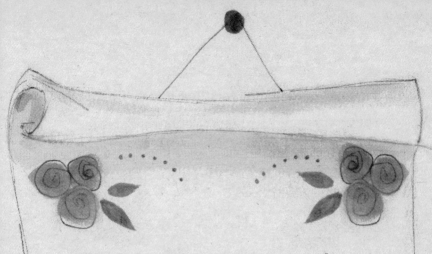

Welcoming Banquet Food Sign-Up

Fairy Sisters	Dish
Jellicoe sisters	~~Tomatoes in aspic~~
	Jelly beans
Flower sisters	~~Roasted broccoli florets~~
	Poppy-seed cake
Seaside sisters	~~Clam chowder~~
	Sand dollar cookies
Curricle sisters	~~Angels on horseback~~
	Pinwheels
Cobweb sisters	~~Silken tofu and carrots~~
	Spun sugar
Oak sisters	~~Acorn squash casserole~~
	Chocolate nut clusters

Only two fairy families had brought what they said they would:

Bakewell sisters   Fairy cakes

Bell sisters   Harmony Casserole

A single Harmony Casserole would never feed an island of fairies plus a colony of gnomes. And much as they all liked sweets, the gnomes and fairies would want something more filling after spending all day outside. *What were they all thinking?* Clara shook her head and smiled a little. *At least we'll have some great desserts.*

Since all of Queen Mab's helpers were at the meadow, any new cooking and preparing would be up to Clara. She looked in the queen's storeroom and was relieved (though not surprised) to see it well stocked.

"This will be a challenge," said Clara. "But I think I'm up to it."

Clara set to work, humming to herself as she rolled up her sleeves and tied on an apron and started washing and sorting.

Before long, pots of water were boiling on the woodstove, vegetables were scrubbed, and eggs were beaten. Clara was putting the finishing touches on a pot of corn chowder when she heard a long, joyous cheer from the meadow. *That will be the end of the opening ceremony*, she thought. *They'll soon be here!*

She felt a gust of icy air come through the door.

"Rosy, is that you? I could really use some help. The fairies have only brought cookies and candies, all because of those silly—"

"Gnomes?" said a deep voice.

Clara turned around. Oh no! A gnome was here—already!

"Hi. I'm Rowan."

"Oh, hello," said Clara.

Clara remembered Rowan well from last year's Games. He had done such a good job! He'd taken fourth place among all the competitors. The two Curricle sisters had won the second and third prizes. Only one other gnome—a brazen young chap called Alasdair who'd come first—had done better than Rowan.

Clara wasn't sure what to say to Rowan. She hadn't ever really talked to a gnome before.

"Um, do you . . . do you remember who I am?" Rowan asked at last. "I was at the Games last year." He blushed. "You were in the, um . . . third row, second from the left when the Games began. You were giving out snacks to the fairies and explaining scoring to your sisters and looking after a little baby. All at the same time."

"Sounds like me."

"You're Clara Bell."

Clara's eyes widened. She wanted to reply, but she wasn't sure what to say. Rowan must have thought that meant she didn't remember who he was, because he added quickly, "I didn't win. I'm sure you remember that."

"You came in fourth," said Clara. "That's a pretty big honor."

"Not if you ask my big brother Alasdair."

"Alasdair's your big brother?" asked Clara.

"Yes, and he never lets me forget it," said Rowan. "He took first prize last year. As usual. But I'm going to beat him this year. I've been training all fall."

"Training? What have you been doing?"

Rowan told Clara all about how he'd been practicing for the Games—running up his own island's steepest hill, lifting boulders, swimming around the Outer Islands.

"But I'm talking too much!" said Rowan. "I'm sorry. Tell me about you, Clara."

Clara hesitated. But she felt Rowan would be very easy to talk to. Maybe it was because she knew he'd soon go back to the Outer Islands and she'd never see him again. Maybe it was the friendly twinkle in his dark eyes. "I've been training, too," she said.

"For the Games?" asked Rowan.

"No, my sister Sylva has been training for the Games. I've been training . . ." Clara stopped herself. She wished she had not brought it up. "Um, did you know we have a baby dolphin in Sheepskerry Bay?"

"Are you changing the subject? Because I have a feeling I know what you've been training for," said Rowan. "I think you're coming into your magic powers."

Clara was startled. How did he know?

"Gnomes can do one or two tricks when they're my age, but they don't get their full powers till they're much older," said Rowan. "Tell me what it's like."

Rowan was so friendly, and Clara was so eager to talk about what was happening to her, that she found herself telling him all about her newfound magical powers. She even related the story of the grasshopper . . . and what Queen Mab had said so many years ago.

"'A very great fairy,'" said Rowan. "Now that is an honor."

"Maybe she says that to every fairy, just to build confidence."

"But that wouldn't be true. Not every fairy becomes a truly great fairy. So I don't think it would be very queenly of her, would it?"

"I suppose not," said Clara. "But how did you guess that my powers were coming? Does it show somehow?"

Rowan busied himself stirring the soup Clara had made, though it didn't really need stirring. "You just look more grown-up than you did last year," he said. "Even prettier."

They heard a clatter behind them, and Rosy burst through the door. "Clara! Julia Jellicoe told me what went on with the banquet. Do you need some help?"

"We're almost all set, Rosy. Rowan here has been helping out." *And guessing things about me I thought nobody knew.* "If you two just finish up, I'll decorate the banqueting hall."

"There's not a lot of time," said Rosy. "Everyone will be arriving in a minute."

"I've got a plan," said Clara.

Clara flew into the banqueting hall. The pine tables were scrubbed, the napkins were pressed, and the tables were set for the welcoming banquet. It looked very simple and very plain.

"That's all very well for a colony of gnomes," said Clara to herself. "But for fairies . . . it lacks a certain sparkle."

Then she recited her charm.

Turn thrice around.
Fling wide your arm.

Sparkle now!
Obey my charm!

She spun around carefully and opened her eyes, hoping for anything but soot. "Oh my!" she cried.

The sparkle charm was different in the palace than it had been on the hill, but the effect was just as beautiful. Where there had been bare floors and empty vases, there were carpets of flowers and pots of blossoms. The tables were covered with spun gold. Balloons and ribbons streamed from the ceiling, and tiny glowing fairy lights sparkled like stars.

"Oh, it's gorgeous!" said Rosy when she flew in to see it. "How did you get all this done so quickly?"

"She works fast," said Rowan. Then he smiled at Clara. "Though it looks a wee bit like magic to me."

Seven

"Tug! TUG! T—U—G!"

Alasdair's team was winning the tug-of-war, and Goldie was almost out of her seat with excitement.

It was the morning after the welcoming banquet. Clara had saved the day.

"You were very smart to make us all some real food," Julia Jellicoe had told her. "Sorry we didn't bring the tomatoes."

Clara smiled. The banquet had worked out perfectly, even if it did wear her out more than she thought it would. There was piping-hot food (helped along by Rosy and Rowan), and everybody was thrilled with all the desserts. The dining hall itself was as magnificent as it had ever been—thanks to Clara's magic. Queen Mab had given Clara a warm smile when she saw the decorations. *Maybe she knows?* Clara thought.

Fairies and gnomes alike had enjoyed themselves enormously. They'd all had a good night's rest, and now the Games were in full swing.

"Come on, Alasdair! Win it for me!" Goldie cried.

With an enormous last PULL, Alasdair's team of gnomes yanked the other team across the centerline and won the contest. "Hooray!" Goldie cheered. Alasdair waved at Goldie in the stands. "I'm fainting!" said Goldie.

"You are such a goose!" said Sylva. "He doesn't really care about you. Look—now he's waving at Iris Flower."

Poppy, in the seat next to Sylva, beamed. "I think he likes Iris too," she said.

"Alasdair is a little show-offy," said Rosy.

"He's not show-offy. He's just the best."

"We'll see about that, Goldie," said Clara. "Alasdair is doing well, but the other gnomes are right behind him." She looked at the scoreboard. Alasdair was in first place; Rowan was a distant fifth. *Come on, Rowan*, she thought. *You can do it.*

eight

All that day, gnomes and fairies played in the Valentine's Games together. The fairies laughed and laughed as the gnomes tried to sprint against them (of course flying is faster than running!), but the gnomes got their own back when they competed in Tossing the Branch. Twelve gnomes and fairies each balanced a huge branch on the palms of their hands, and then tossed it as high and far as they could. Alasdair was the winner of that contest, too, but Rowan was a close second.

The most fun was the three-legged race.

Queen Mab enchanted the leaves on the trees so that each one magically displayed the names of a pair of fairies or gnomes. When the queen said, "Leaves, fall upon us!" the green leaves on the enchanted trees of Lady's Slipper Field cascaded down.

"I'm teaming up with . . . Poppy!" said Sylva. "Queen Mab really knows what to do with her magic. I bet she thinks we'll win!"

"Don't be so sure, Poppy," said Clara. "These gnomes are awfully good."

"Look," said Goldie, with a frown on her face, "my leaf says I'm with . . . Ethelrood." She wrinkled her nose as she looked at the scoreboard. "Ethelrood? What kind of a name is that? And he's in tenth place!"

"Ethelrood is a very old and respected gnomish name," said Clara.

"*Humph!*" said Golden.

Clara didn't want to look at the enchanted leaf that had fallen in her lap. *Maybe I'll be paired with Ro—*

"Clara!" Iris Flower exclaimed. "We're a team!"

She looked at her leaf. Sure enough, it bore the names *Clara* and *Iris*. "We'll be a great team," she told her friend, and she meant it.

"Rosy got Squeakie!" cried Sylva. "They're racing in the baby-stroller lanes with the other baby fairies and their big sisters. And Alasdair is partners with his brother." Sylva paused. "What's his name—Owen."

"His name is Rowan," said Clara.

Queen Mab's clear voice rang out over Lady's Slipper Field. "Racers, prepare!"

"Come on, Sylva!" called Poppy.

And with that, the meadow was festooned with velvet ribbons to tie the racers' legs together.

"Grab a couple of ribbons, Poppy. We'll show those gnomes who can win a three-legged race!"

Queen Mab had changed the rules this year and paired some gnomes and fairies together, so the three-legged races, usually a competition of practiced skill and coordination, turned into a bit of a dog's dinner. A mess, in other words.

There were three races and three prizes in all. In the first race, several fairy-and-gnome pairs ended up laughing so hard they never made it to the finish line. Including Goldie and Ethelrood.

"He's kind of cute!" Avery whispered to Goldie as they'd passed her on the sidelines.

In the second race, Rosy and Squeakie didn't

even know whether they'd crossed the finish line, but they had such fun in the stroller

lane that they didn't care. And Clara and Iris,
who had been friends for such a long time, ran
swiftly together and came in a very respectable
fourth, beating Andy and Hamish, two of the
more popular gnomes.

Soon it was time for the last race.

"Line up!" cried Sylva. "Line up, everybody!"

Rowan and Alasdair clomped down to the
starting line. Sylva and Poppy took their place
next to them.

"Bet we beat you!" said Sylva with a broad smile.

"May the best pair win!" said Rowan, smiling back. "And no flying!"

"We'll see who's best," said Alasdair. And with that, Lady Courtney, the queen's attendant, called "Ready . . . steady . . . GO!" and they were off.

Clara watched, holding her breath, as the race started. She wanted to root for Rowan, but she had to cheer for her sister, too. Poppy and Sylva ran well together. Their legs were the same length; their stride was long; they even breathed together (and they didn't use their wings!). They pulled ahead early, and it was clear they were going to win until—

"No!" cried Clara. A branch caught Poppy's foot, and she tumbled down, taking Sylva with her.

Rowan and Alasdair raced ahead as Poppy

and Sylva sprang to their feet. They were just five yards from the finish line.

The meadow rang with cheers. "Go, Alasdair!" cried the gnomes.

"Go, Sylva! Go, Poppy, go!" cried the fairies.

As if they were one fairy, Sylva and Poppy got back on track, hit their stride, and raced toward the finish line.

The roar from the crowd was tremendous. "You can do it, fairies! You can do it!" With one last surge of strength, Sylva and Poppy crossed the finish line . . . just one wing's width in front of Alasdair and Rowan.

"Hooray!" cried the fairies, and they flapped their wings for joy.

"Well done, Poppy," said Rowan, when he caught his breath. "And you, too, Sylva. Are you all right? That was quite a fall you took."

"Ha!" said Sylva. "That was nothing."

"We still got fifteen points!" said Alasdair.

"But you beat us fair and square," said Rowan. Then he looked around at the crowd. "You're . . . um, Clara's sister, aren't you?"

"Yes," said Sylva. "I'm the youngest Bell sister, except for baby Squeak."

"You sisters really get along well together, don't you?"

"Of course we do!" Sylva laughed. "Except when Goldie teases me too much. Then we're glad to have Clara there—she takes care of us all."

nine

Later that afternoon, as the other gnomes and fairies enjoyed an enchanted snack (fairy doughnut holes!), Clara flew away from the sunny meadow. The competitions were over for the day, and there'd be just enough time for her to try out some more magic.

Clara set her wings eastward and made the long flight up to Sunrise Hill. It was very cold out, but she loved the sting of the wind on her cheeks. It made her feel so alive—as if there was nothing she couldn't do.

An elegant mother deer crossed Clara's path

and looked at her curiously
with its big brown eyes.
Clara walked over to her
and gently touched the tip
of her nose. Deer are very
friendly on Sheepskerry,
and Clara knew this doe from last year's harsh
winter, when she had helped the finicky mother
deer find delicious beechnuts to eat. "Do you
need some more food to eat, Doe-deer?" asked
Clara. "I wish I could magic some up for you."

The sound of trampling startled them both,
and the mother deer bounded away. Clara
turned quickly. Maybe it was a bear!

But it wasn't a bear at all.

"Rowan!" Clara said.

Rowan Gnome stood in front of Clara.
Gnomes cannot fly, of course, so Rowan had
clamped on his ice shoes and taken the slippery
path to the top of the hill. Fairies don't mind if

the paths are slippery and slick, because they don't need to use them much. (You wouldn't walk on ice, either, if you had wings.)

"What are you doing up here?" asked Clara. She always thought of Sunrise Hill as her own special place, especially when fluffy snowflakes were falling, as they were that afternoon.

"The other gnomes told me about Sunrise Hill. They say it's the highest place on Sheepskerry. That's why I brought my toboggan."

"Ooh, that's a beautiful one," said Clara, "and we hardly ever do any sledding on Sheepskerry. Most fairies prefer to fly."

"This hill is perfect for a toboggan ride," said Rowan. "And this snow is perfect . . . for snowballs."

"Don't you dare," said Clara.

"Oh, I wouldn't think of it," said Rowan. He whistled innocently. "But I may pile up a little snow here, just in case."

Clara beat him to it. She scooped up a handful of snow, smushed it into a ball, took aim—and threw! *Ploop!* Clara's snowball landed on Rowan's shoulder.

"Why, you . . . ," said Rowan. He grinned. "I knew I couldn't trust you." He made an armful of white powder into a big ball. "Watch out, Miss Fairy."

"Can't catch me!" said Clara. "I can fly!"

"No fair!" said Rowan.

Clara had speed and grace, but Rowan could boast an excellent throwing arm. After Clara dodged several well-aimed tosses and Rowan's cap got knocked off a third time (amid a lot of laughing), they called a truce.

"Want to build a snow gnome?" asked Rowan.

"No thanks!" said Clara, her eyes merry. "I'll build a snow fairy."

The two of them got to work rolling snow

and sculpting faces. Rowan went off looking for a pinecone for a pipe. "You have lots of interesting stones on Sheepskerry," he said, picking one up and putting it in his pocket.

"And sea glass, too," said Clara. "Just ask Goldie about her collection. Have you found the right pinecone yet? I'm using twigs for fairy wings."

They worked for a while longer as the snow fell. Soon there was a sturdy snow gnome and a beautiful snow fairy on the top of Sunrise Hill.

"She needs a scarf to keep her warm," said Clara, looking at her fairy. "I'll give her mine." She unwound her purple scarf from her neck and wrapped it around her snow fairy. "Much better," she said.

"My gnome needs a cap, but he's not getting mine, not after I had to rescue it from your snowballs so many times." Rowan looked around him. "Plus, the snow is coming down harder now."

All at once, Clara realized she'd been having so much fun that she hadn't even thought about Rosy and Goldie, Sylva and Squeak. "I'd better get home," said Clara. "What if my sisters need me? They won't even know where I am!"

"We'll send them word, to let them know you're all right," said Rowan. He whistled a low whistle, and the doe Clara had seen earlier came bounding through the snow.

"You can talk to deer?" asked Clara in wonder.

"Och, it's not much of a skill. All of us gnomes can talk to woodland creatures," said Rowan. He cradled the deer's neck in his arms, very gently, and whispered in her ear. The doe bounded off again. "She'll tell Queen Mab. Your sisters will be fine."

"Let's hope so," said Clara. "I worry about them." And she started to fly away.

"Wait, Clara," said Rowan. "Your wings might get bogged down in this squall. Come on the toboggan with me. It'll be the quickest way."

Much as she wanted to fly, Clara knew Rowan was right. She climbed onto the long, slender sled behind him. Suddenly cold, she shivered.

"Here," said Rowan. "Take my scarf."

Clara was too chilled to turn him down. He knotted his old brown plaid knit scarf around her neck.

"Thanks, Rowan," she said.

"Och," he said, "it's nothing." He paused for a moment. "Will you be all right?" he asked.

"I'll be fine," she said.

"Then hold on tight!" he said. "Let's go!"

ten

Swiftly, they raced down Sunrise Hill. Clara laughed as they bumped and slipped and slid their way down the hill. "I've never gone this fast on land before!" she called, her eyes bright. She would have enjoyed the ride even more if she hadn't been so worried about her sisters. When they reached the deep snow at the bottom of the hill, Clara said a hasty good-bye to Rowan. Then she flew toward home.

Under the cover of trees, Clara did not need to worry about snow on her wings. She flew straight to the Bell fairy house. All the way home, she fretted about what she would find there: Rosy overwhelmed, Goldie in tears, Sylva frozen in a snowbank, and Squeak crying her eyes out, frightened and alone. Why couldn't she fly any faster?

Finally, panting and out of breath, she arrived at her beloved fairy house. She burst through the door. "Oh, sisters, sisters, where are you? Are you safe? Are you all right?"

She looked around. She didn't see anyone. Not even Rosy. Not even Squeak!

"Goldie, Sylva—where are you?" she cried. "Rosy! Squeakie! Have I lost you forever?" Then Clara heard a very familiar sound.

"No lolo!"

In front of the fire, in a cozy heap, were Rosy, Goldie, Sylva, and Squeak. Three mugs of steaming hot chocolate were on the toadstool table (plus a special bottle of warm milk for you-know-who). Fluffy white marshmallows were roasting on sticks. The smell of popcorn was in the air. The great room was as warm as toast.

"You're all right?" Clara said. "You knew what to do without me?"

"Of course we're all right," said Rosy. "We've had so much fun! This house was built to last."

"Doesn't Sheepskerry look pretty?" asked Goldie. "Everything's white and fresh."

"Queen Mab herself flew over to see us," said Sylva. "She got a message from a deer!"

"Where were you all this time?" asked Goldie.

Clara hesitated a little. Then she said, "I was up on the top of Sunrise Hill with Alasdair's brother. Rowan."

"Rowan!" said Sylva. "What were you doing all that time with a gnome?"

"Chatting about the Games, I'm sure," said Rosy. She noticed the new scarf around Clara's neck. "He seems like a nice gnome," she said to her big sister.

"He is," said Clara. "I really think he is."

eleven

"The Round-the-Island Swim begins... now!"

All the fairies cheered as Alasdair, Rowan, Hamish, Cam, Andy, Ethelrood, and the other gnomes dived off the dock and splashed into Sheepskerry Bay early the next morning. The fairies didn't generally participate in this race—it wasn't wise to take off their wings for such a long time.

"It must be freezing in that water!" said Sylva. "How do they do it?"

"Queen Mab enchanted the bay," said Rosy.

"She made the water as warm as it is in summertime."

"Even then it's too cold for me," said Goldie, with a shiver.

"Still, I'd like to try a Round-the-Island Swim sometime. I could do it so fast my wings wouldn't even notice they were off my shoulders," said Sylva. "Maybe next year!"

"It's all riding on this!" Lady Courtney announced with gusto. "If Alasdair wins, he takes first prize. But since this event is such a high-scoring one, Rowan or Ethelrood could snatch the trophy away from him. What will be the outcome? Who will win the Valentine's Games?"

All the fairies were crowded at the dock to watch the beginning of the race. They started flying toward the West Shore to follow the gnomes' progress when they heard a shout from Iris Flower.

"Come on, everybody," she called. "Queen Mab sent the Royal Balloon so we can follow the race! It's waiting for us behind Clearwater Cottage! Come on!"

Queen Mab hardly ever brought out the Royal Balloon, but when there was going to be a traffic jam of fairies in the sky, it was the best solution.

The Royal Balloon wasn't really a balloon, but everybody called it that. It was an intricate straw basket, lined with deep blue velvet, that was pulled by a flock of very friendly chickadees who lived on Sheepskerry year-round. The black-capped birds chittered with excitement as the fairies piled in.

"Come on, Sylva!" cried Poppy. "Climb aboard!" Next, her own sisters disappeared into the basket. Clara heard Rosy calling her name. "Clara! Clara, where are you?"

Clara almost floated over to the balloon to

be with her friends . . . but then she thought, *They'll be able to see the whole race from up there, but if I stay closer to shore, I can follow Rowan.* "Go ahead!" she called to Rosy. "Go ahead without me!"

The chickadees whistled to one another, and they lifted the balloon gently into the sky. The fairies could soon spot their favorites.

"Come on, Alasdair," cried Goldie. "He's winning!"

"Is that Ethelrood right behind him?" asked Avery. "He's in second place."

"Where's Andy?" asked Judy Jellicoe.

"I hope they all win!" said Rosy.

"A-blay!" said Squeak.

"Yes, Squeakie," said Rosy. "Hooray!"

Clara did not feel sorry that she wasn't up in the balloon with the other fairies. She was enjoying the race along the shoreline. The pack of swimmers had just passed Little Crab Island

and was heading south to Doe Isle.

There was an old-fashioned megaphone in the balloon's basket, and Lady Courtney used it now. "It's Alasdair in the lead," she announced, "with Ethelrood just behind. Andy and Hamish are going strong. Rowan lags, but his stroke is steady."

"Go, Ethelrood!" called Avery.

"And look, fairies! The school of dolphins is helping them along. Nothing more exciting than to try to outswim a dolphin."

"There's Speedy!" called Sylva.

Climbing over the rocks near Sea Glass Cottage, Clara was urging Rowan on. "Alasdair has pulled out ahead early," she said to a pretty mother cardinal she met on the path, "but I have a feeling Rowan will outpace him."

And indeed Clara was right. As the swimmers rounded Foggy Bottom, Alasdair's fast pace flagged, and Rowan, who had been slow but steady, began to pull ahead. "Go, Rowan, go!" called Clara.

But then the race slowed down.

"What's this?" said Lady Courtney through her loudspeaker. "Are those . . . mermaids in the water? They promised Queen Mab they would not disturb the swimmers!"

"We don't always keep our promises!" sang the mermaids. "Surely you know that by now." Clara watched as the mermaids swirled around the gnomes, making them lose their way in the water. Even the dolphins lost their formation as the mermaids splashed and dashed and kicked. "Over this way!" they sang. "No, here!" They held out charms made of pearls and coral to lure the gnomes off course and cause all kinds of mischief, all the way from Eel Reef to Mermaid Rocks.

Soon, most of the swimmers had gone astray. Hamish was heading back to Doe Isle and Cam

was swimming out to sea. Alasdair joined the
three prettiest mermaids on Seal Rock and
rested for a while. "I'm still going to win," he
called to the fairies in the Royal Balloon. "But
how can I resist a mermaid?"

The one gnome who was not bothered by
the mermaids was Rowan. His strong, steady

stroke took him easily past Mermaid Rocks, toward the shoals of Heart Island. Clara was sure he would win the race—and take the gold prize. But then he, too, stopped swimming suddenly and started treading water.

"What is he doing?" Clara said to herself as she strained her eyes to watch him from the shore. "Have the mermaids enchanted him too?" Rowan didn't appear to be hurt or tired, but he wasn't moving an inch. And now that the mermaids had grown bored of them, the other gnomes were once again on course.

"And the race is back on!" cried Lady Courtney from the Royal Balloon. The fairies whistled and cheered as the swimmers headed north to Ram Island. The Royal Balloon was all but out of sight.

Clara stayed where she was. She could see that Rowan was panting hard in the water. He was swimming over to rest on a shoal. He didn't look hurt or injured, but she couldn't be sure. And he seemed to be dragging something with him. "Shall I fly out to help him, little fellow?" asked Clara as a chipmunk scampered up a chestnut tree. "Do you think he needs me?"

The chipmunk ran halfway up the tree and pointed his nose to precisely where Rowan was in the water.

That was good enough for Clara. She gave a few strong flaps of her wings and took flight to the spot where Rowan had stopped swimming. It was cold out on the bay, but Clara bravely faced the wind. As she got closer to Rowan he waved to her, but without his familiar smile.

"What's wrong, Rowan? Are you hurt?"

Then Clara realized why Rowan had stopped. There, in front of them, was a baby dolphin, caught on the shoals of Heart Island. "Oh no! It's Speedy!" cried Clara. "She got off course. Let's take her back to her pod." Clara landed carefully on the slippery rock where Rowan held the dolphin in his arms.

"It's not as easy as that, Clara," Rowan said. "This wee dolphin is hurt. Take a look at her flank."

There was a deep gash on the baby dolphin's

side. "She must have cut herself on these sharp rocks. I don't think she'll last much longer," Clara said. "Can you call the mother dolphin? The way you called the doe?"

"I already have," said Rowan. "But creatures of the sea don't always understand gnomes. I don't think she could hear me."

"Shall I fly off to get Queen Mab? Her magic could help us."

Speedy's body shivered.

"There's no time," said Rowan.

"Then I'll have to do it," said Clara. "I'll have to try the healing charm." She didn't want to repeat what Queen Mab had said: *It takes life to heal life.*

"Will it not take too much out of you?" asked Rowan. "You told me it's not an easy charm."

Speedy made a tiny sighing sound. Her eyes fluttered. Clara could not just stand by and do nothing. Not when there was a chance she might save the baby dolphin.

"I've got to do it, Rowan," she said. "I've got to try the healing charm."

She could not bring herself to say, *Even if it costs me dearly, very dearly indeed.*

twelve

Rowan closed his eyes. Clara did too. They both put their hands on the baby dolphin. "Now, imagine her all well and safe," said Clara. She thought hard about Speedy swimming away to safety, healthy and free. Then she whispered the charm:

Harm and hurt
And pain no more.
Feel this power,
From my core.

May you be
Sound as a bell.
May my magic
Make you well!

Before Clara could even open her eyes, she heard the raspy breath of the baby dolphin again. She looked down at Speedy's side—the gash was still there. Her charm had failed!

"Why won't it work when it worked before? It's so much more important now," Clara said.

"It's okay, Clara," said Rowan. "You can't do everything. The mother dolphin will be here soon, I'm sure." But he did not sound so sure.

They both looked at the baby dolphin. Her eyes were closing. "We're losing her!" cried Clara. "I've got to try it again."

Clara held out her hand and Rowan took hold of it. "Now," she said, "think of Speedy, safe and healed, and swimming back to her pod.

Think hard, Rowan!" He squeezed her hand, and then let her go.

Clara raised her arms and felt her magic surge through her. Loud and clear she said:

Harm and hurt
And pain no more.
Feel this power,
From my core.

May you be
Sound as a bell.
May my magic
Make you well!

Suddenly, magical sparks flew all around them.

"She's breathing, Clara! She's alive!"

Clara looked down at Speedy's side. The gash had healed without a trace, and her tail flicked.

She took a deep breath. "She's full of life!" Clara said in a hoarse whisper. "We did it, Rowan. We saved her."

"You saved her," said Rowan.

And as if she could understand their language, the baby dolphin did a flip off the shallow shoals and made a dive into the deep water. Then she came up again with a big dolphin grin on her face. Her mother and her aunties in the dolphin pod had found her and come to claim her. All at once, the pod of dolphins skittered on their tails out of the water as a way of saying thank you to Rowan, and especially to Clara.

"We're so happy we could help you," Rowan called to them. "Aren't we, Clara?"

But when Rowan turned to Clara, he saw that all the color had drained from her face.

"What is it, Clara?" asked Rowan.

Clara's wings were white as sheets. Her head hung down. She was trembling all over.

"Clara, what's wrong?"

Clara could only speak in a whisper. "Queen Mab told me, 'It takes life to heal life.' Now I understand what she meant."

"No!" cried Rowan. "Clara! We've got to get you home!"

thirteen

Rowan Gnome was out on a rock in the middle of Sheepskerry Bay with a very ill fairy who had to get to safety. If he plunged into the water with Clara, she might be too weak to get to shore. If he left her there to get help, something terrible might happen before anyone could come to her aid.

"Go, Rowan," said Clara in a low voice. "Leave me here and get some help. It's all you can do. Oh, and your race—"

"That's not important now," said Rowan. "I'm not leaving your side."

The dolphin pod circled around them. Speedy nuzzled Rowan with her nose. "Not now, Speedy!" said Rowan. "Clara already helped you. She needs help now."

Speedy tried again. This time, she made a little nickering noise. The other dolphins joined in.

"What is it, dolphins?" said Rowan. "What do you want?"

Then all at once it was clear to him. *Come ride on our backs*, they seemed to say. *Clara helped us. Now we'll help Clara.*

In a moment, the strongest mother dolphin circled the rock where Clara lay. Rowan climbed onto the dolphin's back and pulled Clara tight behind him.

He paused for a moment. "Will you be all right?" he asked.

This time, she could barely say the words. "I'll be fine."

"Then hold on tight!" he said. "Let's go!"

And through the water they glided toward Sheepskerry.

fourteen

Of course by now, the Fairy Bell sisters had spotted their big sister out in Sheepskerry Bay. The chickadees carrying the Royal Balloon spun around and dropped down to where Clara was borne on the dolphin's back. The mermaids saw them coming and for once made no mischief. In fact, they reached their arms up to steady the basket of fairies.

"Here she is!" called Rowan.

The Royal Balloon hovered just inches above the water. Rowan was almost forgotten as Rosy, Goldie, Sylva, and even baby Squeak helped Clara into the basket.

"They have me now, Rowan," said Clara. "I'll be all right. You could even finish the race if you want."

"The race!" said Rowan.

"Don't use up your strength talking," said Golden. "Take us *home!*"

"To Queen Mab's palace, quickly, birds!" called Lady Courtney. "There's no time to lose!"

"She'll be better off at the palace, Goldie," said Rosy. She was cradling Clara's pale face in her hands. "Queen Mab will know what to do."

"Please go quickly, *please!*" said Sylva. "I'll do everything right from now on, I promise. Just please get Clara better again."

"Jojo!" said Squeak.

And like lightning, the birds flew Clara away.

fifteen

I don't want to keep you in suspense about Clara for too long. I'd like to say that she recovered her strength in the Royal Balloon. Or that she was better once she landed on Sheepskerry soil. Or even when she first arrived at Queen Mab's palace.

But none of that would be true.

Instead, Clara could barely lift her head to thank the birds who flew so fast. She could not manage to smile at Lady Courtney, who carried her through Queen Mab's palace toward one of the inner chambers. She could not even summon the strength to squeeze her sisters' hands when they clustered around her, hoping she might show some sign of recovery. And she did not see Rowan, who forfeited the swimming race and paced back and forth in the Great Hall of the palace, waiting for news.

"Shall we send for Tink?" Rosy asked Queen Mab.

"Tink cannot do anything for Clara now," said Queen Mab. "Clara will have to draw strength from within to heal herself. I will do my utmost to help her." Then she added gently, "Sing her a song so she knows you're outside." And she turned toward Clara's chamber.

Rosy, Goldie, and Sylva lifted their voices in song, and Squeakie swayed in rhythm:

Let the circle be unbroken,
As we wait here, by her side.

Let the circle be unbroken,
We'll abide here, we'll abide.

Queen Mab flew silently into the chamber.

"Dear Clara Bell, you used too much magic, too soon, to help another creature in need. Now you are the one who must heal."

Clara was able to lift her head, just a little. "Do you think I can do it?" she asked.

"I know you can," said Queen Mab. "You will be a very great fairy someday."

Clara turned her head away.

"Or have you forgotten my words?" said Queen Mab.

Clara managed a very small smile. "Never, my queen. Never."

"Then draw from your strength within, Clara Bell. And heal."

Queen Mab raised her arms, and the room was filled with light. She knelt down at Clara's bedside. Then, slowly and carefully, in a deep strong voice, she said:

Harm and hurt
And pain no more.
Strength be with you,
From your core.

For you, Clara,
Do I kneel.
May <u>your</u> magic
Make you heal!

Clara's eyes blinked. Her cheeks flushed with color.

"Come, fairies!" called Queen Mab to the Fairy Bell sisters. "Come help your sister."

Rosy, Goldie, Sylva, and Squeak rushed into the bedchamber.

"You can do it, Clara!"

"You're getting better—I can see it!"

"Coomada, coomada!"

"We love you, Clara! We love you!"

Outside the palace, the fairies and gnomes waiting for news heard a magnificent cheer. Then the windows to the bedchamber were flung open.

"She's all better!" cried Rosy.

"She's smiling!" cried Goldie.

"She did it!" cried Sylva.

"A-blay!" cried Squeak.

And down in the Great Hall, Rowan Gnome rubbed his eyes and blew his nose into his gnomish handkerchief. He would tell anyone who asked that his allergies were acting up, but if you ask me, I'd say there might be another reason why his eyes had welled with tears.

sixteen

Clara had never been as happy as she was at the farewell banquet that night. She felt as healthy as she had ever felt in her life—lighter, and more full of life. Queen Mab took care of all the arrangements for the banquet this time, and the feast was sumptuous. There was a roaring fire in the hearth, and all the gnomes and fairies were dressed in their coziest winter sweaters. Everyone was delighted to be there, and the faces of the Fairy Bell sisters were suffused with joy. Tink sent Clara a get-well card that appeared in the middle of the feast by magic.

"Look!" said Rosy. "The postmark is *Neverland!*"

Inside there was a very special message:

I know you'll already be better when you get this, Clara. Queen Mab was right about you! Hugs and kisses, Tink

Everything would have been perfect, except that Rowan was nowhere to be seen. His friends Cam and Hamish told Clara he'd get there after supper. "He's working on a wee project," said Cam. "He'll be along presently."

When supper was finished, the insect orchestra played a fanfare, and Queen Mab flew up to the palace stage.

"These have been some wonderful Valentine's Games," said Queen Mab. "Fairies and gnomes competed together in our annual contest. Sylva Bell broke a record in Fairy Flight."

She looked at Sylva, and Sylva beamed. "And another record was set in Tossing the Branch, thanks to Alasdair Gnome." Alasdair flexed his muscles and flashed a grin at Iris Flower. "And as to the dramatic ending to the Games, and Clara Bell's magnificent rescue"—Clara wished Rowan were there with her—"we will speak of that in a moment.

"Now," said Queen Mab, "Lady Courtney will help me award the prizes to the top three winners. But before we do, let me say this to our gnomish friends: It is a great honor to have had you here on Sheepskerry. You all showed most impressive skills. We look forward to welcoming you back to next year's Valentine's Games!"

A great roar went up from the crowd.

Lady Courtney hovered next to Queen Mab. "May I begin?" she asked.

"Please do," said the queen.

"In third place," Lady Courtney announced,

"is Ethelrood Gnome, with seventy-four points!" The fairies fluttered their wings, and the gnomes cheered loud and long.

"He's awfully nice," said Avery.

"Alasdair's taller," said Goldie.

"Ethelrood Gnome," said Queen Mab. "You have acquitted yourself honorably and well. Please come forward and accept your prize."

The Stitch sisters had made the prizes for the Games again this year. They had crafted a gorgeous brocade vest for third place, the color of a bronze bell. Ethelrood donned the vest with pride. "I dedicate my win to . . . Avery Pastel!" said Ethelrood.

Cheers and hoots came from the gnomes. Avery flew up to Ethelrood, who was smiling broadly. "Nice work, Ethelrood," she said, with a shy smile.

"You can call me Roody," said Ethelrood, with a grin. "And thanks for thinking I'm cute. I think you're cute, too."

"In second place," said Lady Courtney, "is Sylva Bell, with eighty-five points!"

The cheers began again. Sylva flew up to the stage.

"Here is your prizewinner's cape for second place," she said. And she handed Sylva a forest-green cape shot with silver thread. "An extraordinary achievement for your very first competition."

"Thank you, Queen Mab!" she said. "And I bet you know who I dedicate my Games to: my big sister Clara!" said Sylva.

Clara beamed with pride.

"And in first place," said Lady Courtney in her loud, clear voice, "with ninety-six points . . ."

Iris Flower sighed aloud.

"Gnomes and fairies, please stand for Alasdair Gnome!"

"Hooray for Alasdair!" they cried. "Hooray

for Alasdair Gnome!"

Alasdair mounted the podium. "Thank you, thank you," he said. Then he asked, "Where's my wee brother, Rowan? Where's Rowan Gnome?"

"Hey, Rowan," said Hamish. "Get up front!"

Rowan was all the way at the back of the banqueting hall. His friends pushed him forward.

"There you are, Rowan," said Alasdair. "I wanted you to be here to hear me say . . . I dedicate my first-place win to my brother, Rowan. The bravest gnome in all the land!"

A huge cheer went up from the crowd. The Fairy Bell sisters cheered loudest of all.

Clara flew over to talk to Rowan.

"I'm sorry you gave up your chance of winning for me, Rowan," she said. "You could have beaten Alasdair, you know."

"That's water under the bridge—or under the dolphin," said Rowan, and he grinned. "Maybe next year."

Queen Mab cleared her throat, and the crowd was quiet. "Which leads me to my final announcement," she said. "All of you know of the daring and selfless rescue Clara Bell performed during the Round-the-Island Swim. What many of you do not know is that Clara Bell has come into her magical powers."

There was a murmur of "ooh"s and "aah"s and some "I told you so"s throughout the crowd.

"Clara has powers that I did not realize she would have this early," said Queen Mab. "She achieved something remarkable out on Sheepskerry Bay. It took some life from her, but she restored that life to herself. Rowan Gnome was a hero, too, for getting Clara back to Sheepskerry and safety. Rowan, please come up and take a bow."

The crowd cheered again, and Cam and Andy whistled.

"And Clara Dawn Bell, please come take your place next to me. You are now a truly magical fairy."

seventeen

At first, some fairies thought Clara had not come into her magical powers that night. For Clara's dress did not transform into a golden gown; her hair did not spin into curls; her arms and throat did not shine with jewels. But those who know Sheepskerry, and the fairies who live there, realized that Clara was indeed an enchanted fairy, even if she didn't change on the outside. As she flew up to the stage to take her place next to Rowan, her wings were strong, her path was steady, her eyes sparkled, her smile beamed, and there was a glow about her that comes from magic alone.

Rowan and Clara danced the first dance of the Farewell Banquet together. And they danced all the other dances of the evening together, too.

At the end of that beautiful night, as the tide was turning, the gnomes boarded their boats and said good-bye to the Sheepskerry fairies. As Alasdair flirted (he was asking *all* the fairies for their snail mail addresses) and Ethelrood chatted with Avery, Rowan walked with Clara under the moonlight on Sheepskerry Dock.

"I have something for you," he said. "It's why I was late to the banquet."

Clara looked at what Rowan held out to her.

"It's . . . it's a valentine," he said.

Indeed it was a valentine of sorts, but it wasn't made of shiny paper or delicate lace. It was made of stone.

"This is the stone I found on Sunrise Hill," said Rowan. "It's in the shape of—"

Clara took it from him gently. "It's in the shape of a heart," she said.

"I painted it myself," said Rowan, blushing. "Fairies like pink. At least that's what Hamish and Cam told me."

Clara smiled at the splash of pink on the stone heart. Rowan was a better swimmer than he was a painter.

"Look at the back," said Rowan.

Clara turned it over. Carved into the stone were two little words:

YOU ROCK

"Get it?" said Rowan. "It's a rock and—"

"I get it," said Clara. "And Rowan?" She smiled. "You rock, too."

eighteen

"Here's another one for you, Clara!" said Sylva.

The next morning, the Fairy Bell sisters were opening their valentines over a breakfast of mint tea, crumpets, farmer's cheese, and grapefruit marmalade. They always exchanged their family valentines before heading over to Lady's Slipper Field to give out cards and gifts to others. Clara opened the pretty pink envelope and took out a handmade card from Sylva.

"Don't you love it?" asked Sylva.

"I do," said Clara. She read it aloud:

Roses are red
Violets are blue
Be careful with magic
Whatever you do!
With lots of hugs on Valentine's Day
from your little sister Sylva.

"Oh, Clara will be careful with her magic," said Rosy. "But you are growing up, aren't you, Clara?"

"It's fine if you grow up," said Goldie. "But you'd better not move away from us for a long, long time. Who would help me with my fractions?"

"And who would I have to share my secrets with?" said Rosy.

"And who'd keep me from getting in too much trouble?" said Sylva.

"Squeak!" said Squeak.

They all looked at Clara. "You're not going to leave us, are you, Clara?" asked Sylva.

"I'll tell you one thing," said Clara, "nobody's

going anywhere until these breakfast dishes are done." She grinned. "Sylva, you clear the plates. I'll wash them and Goldie can dry."

"Or they can air-dry," said Goldie.

"And Rosy, you'll get Squeakie into her snowsuit, won't you?"

"I certainly will," said Rosy.

The sisters bustled about, and soon all their work was done. They put on boots and hats and gathered up their valentines to deliver to their fairy friends. Of course Sylva could only find one of her mittens. "I have an extra pair upstairs," said Clara. "I'll be right back."

Clara flew upstairs and quickly found a pair of warm mittens to fit Sylva. Before she went downstairs again, she opened up the top drawer of her dresser. In it was the very special valentine Rowan had given her, wrapped in an old brown scarf. She took it out carefully. The pink paint was already flaking off, but nothing would change the shape of the heart-shaped rock, or what Rowan had written in stone.

"Clara! What are you doing up there?" called Goldie from downstairs. "We can't wait forever."

Clara smiled. "But maybe I will," she said as she put Rowan's heart back where it belonged. "Coming!" she called to her sisters.

She flew down the stairs, linked arms with Rosy, and opened the door to the dazzling day.

fairy secrets

Squeak's Words

A-blay!: Hooray!

Coomada!: Love it!

Jojo!: Hurry!

No lolo: Don't be sad.

Tutu!: Me too!

Squeak!: Oops! or Uh-oh! or Yay! or sometimes, *Yikes!*

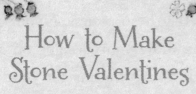

How to Make
Stone Valentines

*These directions can be used
by fairies, gnomes, or children.*

Look in your backyard or in a garden or a park or even a beach for stones.

Stones that are oval, round, or heart-shaped work best.

Try to find stones with a flat surface, as they are easiest to paint.

Take the stones home and scrub them in the sink. Make sure you ask a grown-up to help with this part as stones can be dirty and grimy and not everyone likes to have dirt and grime in their sinks. Once the stones are clean, let them dry completely. Be as patient as you can.

You can draw your designs on a piece of paper while you're waiting for your stones to dry. Or, if you're like Rowan, you can skip the drawing and just go straight to painting.

Find some fairy paint or, if you can't find that, use acrylic or tempera paint to decorate your stones. Acrylic is shinier, but tempera washes off easily. (So if you like to change your mind a lot, use tempera.)

You can decorate your stones with patterns or stripes. You can cover your stone with just one color. Or you can write messages on your stones. Here are Valentine's messages that could fit on a stone:

XOXO

BE MINE

U R CUTE

LUV U

Sometimes fairies write messages and leave them for children to find. Be on the lookout for fairy stones—someday there may be a message waiting for you.

Fairy Bell Sisters' Song

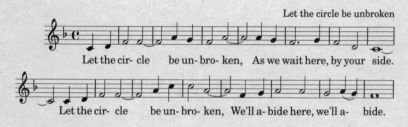

Let the circle be unbroken

Let the cir- cle   be un- bro- ken,   As we wait here, by your   side.

Let the cir- cle   be un- bro- ken, We'll a- bide here, we'll a-   bide.

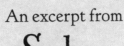

An excerpt from

Sylva
and the
Lost Treasure

The Fairy Bell Sisters

Book 5

Sylva was just about to head sadly back to the Bell fairy house with her one broken button and the cracked teacup when they caught sight of Queen Mab's attendant. Lady Courtney was flying slowly out of the palace, with something very large in her arms.

"Heigh-ho, here's Lady Courtney," said Sylva.

"She'll probably tell us we're not allowed to touch anything," said Poppy.

"Or that we need to curtsy before we approach the jumble pile." They both giggled.

"I think she needs help," said Sylva. "That's a huge crate she's carrying."

The two fairies flew over to Lady Courtney, who was indeed struggling under the weight of a large crate, which looked very old.

"Sylva, Poppy, good afternoon to you," said Lady Courtney.

"May we help you, Lady Courtney?" asked Sylva, using her best manners. "That looks awfully heavy."

"It is heavy," said Lady Courtney. She set the box down with a rattling thump. "Whew! These wings aren't getting any younger."

"Probably a whole box of broken plates and cups," whispered Sylva.

"Plus some dirty old pieces of string," Poppy whispered back. She and Poppy giggled again.

"Are you two the only fairies here?" asked Lady Courtney. "I think you're in luck."

Sylva and Poppy flew over to the crate. It had a latch on the front and opened quite easily. Inside was not a jumble of old rubbish that no one would want. Inside was something so marvelous that Sylva and Poppy could hardly believe it.